HOW I SURVIVED MIDDLE SCHOOL

The New Girl

By Nancy Krulik

SCHOLASTIC INC.
New York Toronto London Auckland Sydney
Mexico City New Delhi Hong Kong Buenos Aires

ISBN-13: 978-0-545-01303-1
ISBN-10: 0-545-01303-8

Published by Scholastic Inc.
SCHOLASTIC and associated logos are trademarks and/or registered trademarks of Scholastic Inc.

12 11 10 9 8 7 6 9 10 11 12/0

Printed in the U.S.A. 40
First printing, September 2007
Book design by Alison Klapthor

For Ian B. and his friends in the RSS Middle School Class of '08. Thanks for the inspiration.

HOW I SURVIVED MIDDLE SCHOOL

The New Girl

What Does Your Locker Say About You?

One of the coolest things about being in middle school is that you have a locker. It's the one place in the whole school where you can do your own thing – and no one has anything to say about it but you. You can keep things neat and orderly, or you can cram so much stuff in there that everything falls out the minute you open the door. It's all up to you because it's your private space. Your locker is a reflection of who you are.

So, just what does the inside of your locker say about your personality? Are you glamorous, dreamy, sporty, or some *combination* of the three? Get ready, because we're about to unlock the answers.

1. You keep an extra pair of shoes at school – just in case you get caught in the rain or step in something gross. What kind of shoes are lurking in your locker?

A. High heels

B. Ballet flats

C. Sneakers

2. What essentials are always on hand inside your locker?

A. Nail polish and lip gloss

B. A romance novel and your diary

C. Hair bands and a bottle of water

3. What do you have taped up on your locker door?

A. A mirror and photos of you hangin' with your friends

B. A photograph of that new hottie from your favorite TV show

C. Your team schedule

4. How do your friends feel about your locker?

A. They know they can stop by any time for a quick mini makeover.

B. They love to hang out nearby because of the sweet-smelling potpourri you keep inside.

C. They know it's the school spirit headquarters.

5. If you were allowed to paint your locker any color (but you're not, so put the spray paint can away!) what would it be?

A. Bright turquoise

B. Pale pink

C. The colors of your favorite sports team

6. What would your friends be most surprised to discover inside your locker?

A. Five shirts and three sweaters — you never know when you're gonna want to change your look in the middle of the day. Besides, you ran out of room in your closet.

B. A love letter to the guy who sits behind you in algebra that you wrote but were too shy to send.

C. Half-full bags of chips and pretzels that you keep on hand, just in case you need a carb rush right before gym class.

7. If your locker could be anywhere in the school, where would you like it to be?

A. Close to the girls' room, so you can dash in and change your outfit midday without having to travel too far.

B. Near a window, so you can get a glimpse at the world outside as you pick up your books for your next class.

C. Either near the cafeteria or the gym, because lunch and P.E. are your favorite hours of the day.

Okay, now it's time to unlock the secrets of your personality.

Mostly A's: You're the glam girl of the gang. Your locker is the style capital of the school. 3

Mostly B's: Every group of girls needs a romantic, and you're the one! No one can deny that you have a soft, dreamy personality that is absolutely irresistible. 2

Mostly C's: Jocks rock! And no one knows that better than you. If there's a game to play, you're the first on the field. Sports are great for your mind and body. 4

Chapter ONE

"JENNY, YOU DROPPED SOMETHING," my good friend Felicia Liguori said, pointing toward a piece of pale pink paper that had fallen out of my locker and landed on the floor.

I started to bend down to pick up the note, but Dana Harrison stomped her high-heeled black boot on top of it before I could grab it. Dana just missed stepping on my fingers. Not that that would have mattered to her.

"Ooh, Jenny McAfee has a note. This I've gotta read," Dana said with more than a hint of sarcasm in her voice. She rolled her eyes in the direction of her friends, Claire and Addie.

"Yeah, I'll bet it's really interesting," Claire joked even more sarcastically.

"Hey, that's private!" I shouted, trying to grab the note away from Dana. But she didn't give it back to me. In fact, my scream made her want to read it even more.

Oh man, I thought to myself as Dana opened up the note. *This isn't going to be pretty.* I could feel the heat rising up in my cheeks.

"Jen-Jen, here are some sugar cookies for my supersweet girl. Good luck on your Spanish quiz. Love, Mommy,"

Dana read aloud. She started to snicker really loudly. "Jen-Jen. Oh, that's hilarious."

"*Super-sweet* Jen-Jen," Addie Wilson added between giggles.

"How nice – a love note from your *mommy*." Claire laughed so hard she actually snorted.

"Give that back to me!" I demanded, grabbing the note back from Dana and shoving it into my jeans pocket. Not that it mattered; they'd already read it. The damage had been done. And even if I tried to act all cool like it didn't matter, the Pops would know it did. The telltale red blush of embarrassment on my cheeks would surely give me away.

As Dana, Claire, and Addie walked off, I sighed and added another item to my ever-growing list of very important rules they don't tell you in sixth grade orientation.

MIDDLE SCHOOL RULE #16:

ALWAYS DESTROY ANY EVIDENCE OF YOUR PARENTS' EXISTENCE BEFORE YOU ENTER THE SCHOOL BUILDING.

Okay, I know that sounds mean. It was really nice of my mom to give me cookies and wish me luck on my test. I love my mom. I really do. It's just that it's so uncool to have anything from your parents with you at school. Oh sure, everyone here knows that we all have parents. It's not like we think we were hatched from eggs or anything.

But whenever anybody mentions doing anything with their parents – or worse, gets notes from them – people are going to make fun of them. Especially the Pops. They make fun of everything.

The Pops. That's what my friends and I call kids like Addie, Dana, and Claire. As in *pop*ular. Because that's what they are: the most popular kids in school. You can spot a Pop from a mile away. They're the ones wearing the coolest clothes, the ones who set the trends for everyone else. Everyone in the school says they hate the Pops, but they all want to be them, too. Even me. I admit it. Once in a while I think it would be great to be one of the kids everyone looks up to. Someone like Addie Wilson.

The hardest part about all this is that Addie and I weren't *always* on opposite ends of the popularity scale. In fact, back when we were in elementary school, we were best friends. Inseparable. We were so tight that you would never find Addie Wilson without Jenny McAfee. It was like we were one person – Jenaddie McWilson.

But that was then. And *this* is now. From the minute Addie and I first walked through the front door of Joyce Kilmer Middle School back in September, everything changed. Sometime over the summer, while I was away at overnight camp, Addie had decided she was too cool to be my friend anymore. Therefore, our friendship was over. And I hadn't had any say in the matter.

But just because I didn't hang out with Addie anymore didn't mean we didn't see each other. We were in a few classes together, and we were both in student government. I was the sixth grade class president, and Addie was vice president. (You can't imagine what a shock it was when I beat Addie out for the presidency. It was like something you only see in the movies: *The Revenge of the Non-Pops*!)

And speaking of the student council, I had been on my way to a meeting when Dana had stopped to read my mother's note out loud. My guess is that was where Addie had been off to as well, since we had our weekly meeting at 3:15. Weekly student council meetings were mandatory if you were class president or vice president.

It would have been nice to walk over to the office with Addie, but I knew that wasn't happening. She'd made it clear that even though we both had to go to all the meetings, we weren't a team or anything. She never sat next to me, and when I made suggestions, she usually rolled her eyes. That was her way of making sure everyone on the student council knew that even though I was the class president, I didn't represent her or any of the other sixth grade Pops.

Even though that hurt, I knew that I did represent a lot of other people. After all, when it came to the war of the Pops vs. the non-Pops, there were a whole lot more of us than there were of them. Like my friend Felicia, for instance. She was always there for me, even when Addie and her friends were being incredibly mean.

"Are you taking the late bus today?" I asked Felicia as I watched Addie and her pals walk off.

"Mmm-hmm," she replied with a nod. "I've got basketball practice all afternoon. Want me to save you a seat?"

"Totally. Or I'll save you one if I get there first." I shoved my history book into my backpack and turned slightly, just in time to see my friend Josh coming down the hall. "I think someone's here to see you," I told Felicia with a grin.

Felicia smiled so broadly, the overhead lights reflected off the wire retainer in her mouth. "Hi, Josh," she said excitedly.

"Hi," Josh replied quietly. Even though everyone in school knew Josh and Felicia had been boyfriend and girlfriend since practically the first week of school, he was still a little shy about it. "Hey, Jenny," he added.

"Hey, Josh." I looked up at the clock on the wall. Three-thirteen. Yikes! I only had two minutes to get to the student council office, which was all the way on the other side of the school. "I'm not being rude or anything, but I've gotta go," I told him.

"You'd better hurry," Felicia said. "If you're not there to stop her, Addie's liable to declare herself supreme ruler of the school before the meeting even starts."

I laughed. That was a joke, but it had more than just a ring of truth to it. Addie did have a tendency to take over. But that was probably because people usually let her. Such is the power of the Pops.

* * *

All of the other class representatives were seated by the time I reached the student council office. As I took my seat, Sandee Wind, the eighth grade class president, pulled out a sheet of paper. "I think you all know about the earthquake that destroyed those towns in South America," Sandee began.

I nodded. There was no way we could have missed it. It had been on the news for days, and everyone had discussed it during the current events part of their history classes.

"Well, Ms. Gold has suggested that our school raise money to help the kids at some of the schools that were destroyed," Sandee continued.

Ms. Gold is our school principal. When she suggests something, it's more of an order than a request. But that was okay in *this* case. Helping kids who were affected by the earthquake was really important.

"Do they need textbooks?" Ethan James, the seventh grade vice president, asked. "Because I'd be glad to send my math book."

Sandee giggled. "I think Ms. Gold had a fund-raiser in mind. They need money more than anything else down there."

Addie stood up and smiled at all the class representatives. "I think we could raise a lot of money by having a school dance. The last one was a *huge* success. So many people came. I'd be glad to be in charge . . . again."

Now it was my turn to roll my eyes. Addie and I had

both been in charge of the last school dance. She seemed to have forgotten that small point. Of course, so had everyone else.

"The last dance *was* amazing," Sandee complimented Addie. "You really know how to throw a party."

"But that dance was just a few weeks ago," John Benson, the eighth grade vice president, pointed out. "I think we need to do something new. Something bigger and even better."

Addie frowned. Obviously she didn't think anything could be bigger or better than a dance she was in charge of.

"How about a school carnival?" Kia Samson, the seventh grade president, suggested. "You know, with different game booths and prizes. We could have it on the field behind the school."

"That sounds fun," I piped up. "Everybody loves carnivals. And that way we could raise even more money, because we could invite our parents and brothers and sisters. We couldn't do that if we had a dance."

"Seriously," Kia agreed. "Who'd want to go to a dance with their parents?"

"But a dance is inside," Addie pointed out. "What if it rains on the day of the carnival?"

"We'll set a rain date," Kia told her.

"We wouldn't need a rain date for a dance," Addie countered. "And I bet I could get the same band to play again."

"That band was pretty cool," Sandee agreed.

I couldn't argue with Addie on that count. Addie

had managed to get a high school band to play at our last dance – for free. Even the eighth graders had been impressed with that.

But that didn't mean I wanted Addie to be in charge of another school project. Besides, I thought the carnival was a better idea. And I suspected most of the other representatives felt the same way. "Why don't we vote on it?" I suggested.

"The sixth grade president has called for a vote," Sandee said, trying to sound very official. "All in favor of a school dance, raise your hands."

Addie's hand shot up into the air. Sandee raised hers, too.

"All in favor of a carnival, raise your hands," Sandee said.

John, Kia, Ethan, and I all raised our hands high.

"Carnival it is," Sandee declared. "Kia, since this was your idea, why don't you take charge? We should probably plan to have the carnival soon, because they desperately need money down there. Can you get it together really fast?"

Kia nodded. "I'll start printing up flyers and getting a committee together right away." She looked around the table. "It would be great if each of you could get your friends together to plan a booth as soon as possible."

I grinned. This was going to be fun. My group of friends was so creative, I was sure that we could come up with something really incredible.

Addie, however, wasn't grinning at all. She obviously wasn't pleased that someone else was in charge of the fund-raiser. And from the dirty look she was giving me, it was clear she wasn't too happy that I'd voted for the carnival instead of her dance. So it was no surprise that as soon as the meeting broke up, Addie cornered me in the hallway.

"I can't believe you voted against me," Addie said, her blue eyes narrowing into little angry slits. "We *both* represent the sixth grade. I thought we were a team."

Since when? I thought. But I didn't say that. There was no sense making Addie angrier than she already was. "I just thought it might be fun to try something new," I told her.

"I suppose you'll be building your booth with those people you eat lunch with," Addie said.

Something in the way she said "those people" really made me angry. Like we were beneath her or something. Which we definitely were not.

"I hope so," I told her. "My friends have great ideas. I know we're going to have an awesome booth."

"Are you sure?" Addie asked me.

"Totally," I replied confidently.

"Well, I'm sure *my* friends and I are going to have the hottest booth at the whole carnival," Addie countered boldly. She paused for a moment. "In fact I'm so sure, I'm willing to bet on it."

"Huh?"

"I'm willing to bet you that our booth will earn more money for the earthquake victims than yours will," Addie repeated.

"Okay," I agreed with a shrug. "It's a bet." I started to walk away.

"Not so fast," Addie said, stopping me. "We haven't bet anything yet."

Uh-oh. I didn't like the sound of that. "What should we bet?" I asked, trying not to sound too nervous.

"Something good. *Really* good," Addie said. She thought for a second. "I've got it! The loser has to wear her pajamas to school for a whole day. And not under her clothes, either. She has to wear them so the whole school can see them."

I gulped. Wearing pajamas to school would break another unspoken Middle School Rule.

MIDDLE SCHOOL RULE # 17:

DON'T DO ANYTHING THAT WILL MAKE YOU STAND OUT TOO MUCH FROM THE CROWD. PEOPLE MAY NEVER FORGET AND IT WILL FOLLOW YOU FOR YOUR ENTIRE MIDDLE SCHOOL CAREER.

"P . . . pajamas?" I repeated. I didn't like the sound of that.

Addie nodded. "Oh, yeah. Tops *and* bottoms," she said. "No nightshirts that look like regular shirts, and no saying that you always sleep in sweatpants. Because I know you don't."

That was true. Addie and I had had enough sleepovers in the past to know that we both slept in flannel pajamas – tops and bottoms.

I thought about this for a minute. I was pretty sure my friends and I could come up with a really cool carnival booth. But would it be cool enough to make more money than a booth run by the Pops?

"Well?" Addie demanded.

I looked at Addie. She seemed really confident – like the Pops could never lose at something like this. She was probably right. But it still made me angry to see her so sure of herself. So, despite my fear of forever being known as Pajama Girl, there was only one thing I could say.

"It's a bet."

Chapter TWO

"A CARNIVAL?" My friend Rachel's voice scaled up excitedly as she, Felicia, and I met up in the school parking lot to wait for the late bus. Rachel was on the basketball team with Felicia, so she had stayed late at school, too. And now I could tell she was glad she had. This was big news.

"How cool is that?" Felicia asked her. "The first ever Joyce Kilmer Middle School carnival."

"And we're the only ones who know about it," Rachel added excitedly.

"We're going to have all kinds of game booths and prizes and . . ." I began to explain.

But Rachel interrupted me. "This reminds me of a joke."

Felicia and I sighed. What *didn't* remind Rachel of a joke?

"It's about two cannibals who go to a carnival," Rachel continued. "They play a few games, and then they get kinda hungry. So they start eating one of the clowns. And after a few bites, one cannibal turns to the other and says, 'Does this taste funny to you?' "

I giggled a little, just to make Rachel feel good. But Felicia didn't even bother.

"That was a real groaner, Rach," she said.

"Yeah, but the *carnival* is going to be awesome," I said, bringing the conversation back to the important stuff. "And we have to come up with the best booth."

"*Have* to?" Rachel asked. "Why?"

I was just about to tell them about the pajama bet when Addie walked by on her way to the late bus. I didn't want Addie to think I was worried or anything. So I just smiled and said, "I'll tell you about it later."

Rachel and Felicia looked at me strangely.

"I promise, I'll call you guys tonight and explain," I assured them. "I can't wait to get started."

"Get started on what?" Chloe Samson asked as she walked over to join us.

I had to laugh when I saw the T-shirt Chloe was wearing. It read:

I can only be nice to one person a day.
Today's not your day.
Tomorrow's not looking good, either.

Of course her T-shirt wasn't very accurate. The truth was, Chloe was nice to a lot of people. In fact, she was the first person at Joyce Kilmer Middle School to come over and introduce herself to me. She was also the one who had asked me to have lunch at her table, which was where she introduced me to almost all of my new friends. I would always be grateful to her for that.

"How was play practice, Chloe?" I asked her.

"Fine," Chloe replied quickly, obviously annoyed that I'd changed the subject. Chloe hated it when she didn't know what was going on. "Get started on *what*?"

"Our booth," Felicia told her. "For the school carnival."

"We're having a carnival?" Chloe asked, surprised.

Rachel nodded. "In three weeks. But they're not announcing it until tomorrow. We just know about it because the class president is our pal."

"It's good to have friends in high places," Felicia agreed.

Chloe grinned. "Well, I have a secret, too," she said mysteriously. "A good one."

"A secret?" I asked excitedly. Chloe had definitely piqued my interest. "What is it?"

"Yeah, come on," Felicia added. "Give it up."

"It wouldn't be a secret if I told you, would it?" Chloe pointed out.

I smiled. I knew Chloe wouldn't be able to keep her secret for very long. She never could. We'd know all about it in a few seconds.

Sure enough, I was right. A moment later, Chloe was pulling us in real close to her, so we could hear her when she whispered. "There's a new kid starting school tomorrow," she said.

"A new kid?" I asked.

Chloe nodded. "I heard Ms. Gold talking about some new sixth grader named Sam on the phone."

"Sam, just like your mouse," Rachel teased me. I smiled. Sam was the name of one of my two pet mice. The other one was Cody.

"I hope the new kid's cuter than *your* Sam," Felicia said to me.

"My Sam is cute," I insisted.

"For a mouse," Felicia agreed. She turned to Chloe. "Is the new kid Sam like in Samuel, or Sam like in Samantha?"

Chloe shrugged. "I think Samantha. I'm pretty sure Ms. Gold said 'she' at one point."

"So where's she from?" Rachel wondered. "Another city? Another state?"

"Why is she switching schools in the middle of the year?" Felicia asked.

Chloe shrugged again. "I've already told you everything I know."

I could tell Chloe was getting annoyed with Felicia and Rachel's questions, questions Chloe didn't have the answers to. That was the kind of thing that really bugged Chloe. She liked having all the answers. So I was really glad to see the buses pull up. "Hey, the buses are here," I pointed out. "I'll talk to you guys tonight about the carnival," I told Rachel and Chloe as I started to pull Felicia toward our bus.

"I'll call *you*," Rachel said. "I'll conference everyone in."

"Sounds good," I said. "About eight?"

"You got it," Rachel said. "At eight. Won't be late."

And she wasn't. Sure enough, my cell phone rang at eight o'clock on the dot.

"Hello!" Three voices greeted me as I answered my phone.

"Hi, guys," I replied to Chloe, Rachel, and Felicia.

"Now tell us what's so important about having the best booth," Felicia said. "It obviously has something to do with Addie. You sure clammed up the minute she walked by."

I frowned. I was kind of hoping Felicia and Rachel had forgotten I'd said anything like that. I really didn't want to have to tell them about the incredibly stupid bet I'd made. Because the more I'd thought about it, the more I knew I'd be the one in flannel pajamas and slippers come the Monday after the carnival. There was no way we were going to make more money than the Pops, no matter what kind of booth we had.

"Yeah, spill," Rachel added.

I was going to have to tell my friends what I had done. So spill I did. About everything – the way Addie had looked so smug, and how she'd practically dared me to bet her. And when I was finished with the story there was dead silence on the phone. At least for a minute. Then, finally, Chloe said, "Okay, so we'll beat them, that's all."

She made it sound so simple, so *possible.* I laughed. That was so Chloe. She was nothing if not optimistic. "How are we going to do that?" I asked her.

"Well, I have an awesome idea for a booth," Chloe said. "Something everyone in the whole school will want to try."

I could feel Rachel and Felicia's excitement burning through the phone lines. I was pretty stoked, too. Chloe really sounded like she was on to something.

"We'll have a karaoke booth!" she said.

I sighed. *Or not.* "Chloe, not everyone likes to sing as much as you do," I reminded her.

"Sure they do. Karaoke is the hottest thing right now," Chloe insisted. "All the movie stars are doing it."

"That doesn't mean kids at our school are going to pay money to sing out loud," Felicia told her. "Most of us would actually be pretty embarrassed to do that."

"For sure," Rachel echoed. "We don't have too many movie star-like people in our school."

"Just *future* movie stars," Chloe said with a giggle. "Like me."

I grinned. Chloe was definitely the queen of positive thinking. "I wish I had your confidence," I complimented her.

"Some things you just know," Chloe explained.

"I wish I knew what kind of booth to make," I said.

"We should change the subject," Felicia said. "Then maybe an idea will just come to us."

"Okay," I agreed – since even I was tired of stressing over the carnival. "How about a quiz?"

"Cool!" Felicia said.

"Oh, yeah, that would be fun," Chloe agreed.

"Can you find a good one?" Rachel asked.

I was pretty sure I could. I went over to my computer and logged on to my favorite website, www.middleschool survival.com. I had accidentally stumbled upon it when I was miserable and friendless after Addie dumped me for the Pops. It has articles and advice, and there are tons of quizzes about fashion and friends. So far, the quizzes on the site had helped me figure out whether or not I should run for class president (which I did, obviously), whether Addie and I would ever be BFF again (not gonna happen), and if my new friends were true blue (totally!).

"Oh, here's a perfect one," I told the girls. "It's made for you, Chloe. It's called *Is There Fame in your Future?*"

"Oh, let's do it!" Chloe squealed with excitement. I had to laugh. Chloe sure loved being the center of attention. But that was okay. It was one of the things I liked best about her.

"Are you destined for the red carpet?" I read into the phone. *"Should you be practicing signing your autograph and getting your Oscar speech ready? Answer these questions, and see what the future holds for you."*

"Okay, I'm ready!" Chloe answered.

I began to read the questions.

If someone starts a rumor about you, do you:

A. Go all over the school denying it. You can't have people telling lies about you – it might hurt your reputation. And even if it doesn't, it hurts you.

B. Feel flattered that people are talking about you. After all, there's no such thing as bad publicity. Let people think what they will. You know the truth.

"Oh, I know exactly what you'd do, Chloe," Rachel said. "Absolutely nothing. You'd just let people think whatever they wanted to. That's what you did when that Madame X column came out."

We all remembered the Madame X episode. Addie had been anonymously spreading rumors in the school newspaper through a gossip column. She'd called herself Madame X. One of the rumors Addie'd started had been that Chloe had a secret boyfriend. It wasn't true, though. We all thought Chloe would get mad about the rumor but she hadn't. She just laughed.

"You're right," Chloe said. "I would choose B."

"Okay, next one," I said, as a new question popped up on the screen.

Where's your fave spot at a school party?:

A. Right next to the nicest guy in your grade – a quiet chat is usually what you're in the mood for.

B. In the middle of the dance floor getting your groove on. You love being the center of attention.

"CENTER OF ATTENTION!" Rachel, Felicia, and I all shouted at once.

"Who, me?" Chloe joked. But she didn't deny it. How could she?

"That's B again," I said, clicking on it. "Next question."

When you have some spare cash, what do you do?

A. Put it in the bank. You're saving up for something special.

B. Head directly to the mall – it's time for a shopping spree!

"Totally A," Chloe said. "Ever since my dad's been out of work, I save every bit of baby-sitting money I can. I don't want to have to ask my mom for anything. Besides, I'm just not that into clothes."

That was true enough. Chloe's whole wardrobe basically consisted of overalls, jeans, and T-shirts. I clicked the letter A.

"Okay, how about this one?" I asked.

You and a friend bump into some of her camp friends at the local diner. Your pal is so caught up in the spontaneous reunion she forgets to introduce you. How do you handle things?

A. Elbow your friend in the side as a gentle reminder that you'd like her to clue her camp buddies in to who you are.
B. Step right up, stick out your hand, and make your presence known.

"Oh, Chloe *always* makes her presence known," Felicia said. Chloe laughed.

That was for sure. Who else would dance through the cafeteria on a rainy day singing "*The sun will come out, tomorrow*?"

"B it is," I said. "Now here's the last one."

What does your dream house look like?
A. A two-story house, complete with swimming pool and a nice big yard.
B. A fancy apartment in New York City with a view of Central Park.

"New York! Definitely New York!" Chloe squealed excitedly. "I've always wanted to go there. I would die to see a Broadway show. Or better yet, be in one."

"Well, you're already a drama queen," Rachel teased, noting the overabundance of excitement in Chloe's voice.

I clicked the letter B. The screen darkened for a minute as the computer tallied up Chloe's score. "You answered four B's and one A," I told her as the results popped up on the screen. "Let's see what that means." I scrolled down and read from the website.

If you answered mostly A's, the crystal ball doesn't seem to show fame in your future. You're more of a behind-the-scenes, down-to-earth kinda gal. And that's okay. After all, fame can be fleeting. But a strong sense of self, and a knowledge of what's important in life, will stick with you forever.

"But I had way more Bs than As," Chloe reminded us. "So what does that mean?"

I giggled. Chloe had absolutely no patience. Finally I gave her the answer she'd been hoping for.

Mostly B's: Get ready for your close-up! You know where the spotlight is, and you're an expert at getting it to shine on you. Fame is on the way. Just remember, the people who knew you before you were famous are the ones who will always be your BFFs! Treat them kindly.

"Yeah, always remember us, the little people," Felicia teased.

We all laughed. The idea of Felicia – who was the tallest girl in our grade and on the varsity basketball team – being called little was hilarious.

"I'll never forget you," Chloe said. "What were your names again?"

"Very funny." I laughed. Then, suddenly, I stopped. I had just remembered something not so funny. "No one is ever going to be able to forget the sight of me walking down the hall in my pj's," I groaned.

"It's not going to come to that," Chloe assured me. "We'll think of something, Jenny. You'll see."

"We don't have to decide tonight, do we? We have time to think about it, right?" Rachel asked.

"Yeah, a few days anyway. I have to let Kia know what we plan to do soon though," I told her.

"Maybe that new girl will have an idea," Chloe suggested, reminding us all that she'd had some big news today, too. "I wonder if Sam's smart."

"Or athletic," Rachel added.

"Or nice," I chimed in.

"I guess we'll find out all about her tomorrow," Felicia said. "We're just going to have to wait and see."

Chapter THREE

I WAS ONE OF THE FIRST ones to meet Sam the next morning because we were in the same English class. Before class began, Ms. Jaffe stood up and walked to the front of the room with Sam by her side.

"Class, this is Samantha Livingston," Ms. Jaffe said. "I trust you will all welcome our new student in the nicest way possible. After all, each of you was new to Joyce Kilmer Middle School just a few short months ago."

That kind of introduction would have made me blush. I hate being in front of the class for any reason, but to be the new girl, standing there while the teacher practically forced people to be kind to me, would have just about killed me.

But Sam didn't seem the least bit uncomfortable. That was the *first* thing I noticed. The second was that this new girl didn't dress at all like the rest of us. Her dark brown hair was cut at an angle and straight, and she even had a small hot pink streak in it! It was really cool – no one else at our school had a hairstyle like it. Her clothes were really different, too. I had never seen anything like her black-and-white T-shirt with red-and-blue graffiti splashed on it. There wasn't a shirt like that in any of the stores in our mall. Not even at the trendiest boutiques.

I had a feeling that wherever Sam was from, it was pretty far from here. She sure didn't dress like anyone in our hometown.

"Hello, Sam." Our class greeted the new girl in unison.

"Cheers, everyone," Sam replied in a posh English accent. "I'm so excited to be in the States."

The States. Somehow that sounded so much cooler than just saying "America." It had that European sound to it, which made perfect sense, since England was in Europe. I looked at Sam's hair and clothing with a new eye. She didn't look odd or different to me anymore. She just looked stylish and sophisticated. Very European.

Which, in our school anyway, meant that Sam was destined for life as a Pop. They were sure to scoop up this new girl immediately. She was just their kind.

I looked over at Chloe. She was already opening her grammar textbook and pulling out a pen. Obviously she'd realized the same thing – there was no sense getting too excited over Sam. She was headed for a different crowd.

By lunchtime, it was clear that my prediction had come true. Sam was seated across the cafeteria, at the round table near the windows. *The Pops table.* And by the way she was smiling and giggling, it seemed as though Sam's initiation into the Pops' world had gone really smoothly.

But there was no time to consider how Sam had managed to do in three hours what so many of the other kids in the school hadn't been able to do in three months. I had a bigger issue to deal with – the pajama drama that I was now in the middle of.

"Okay, so we have to have the most incredible booth," I urged my friends.

"I don't understand how you could let Addie talk you into making a stupid bet with her anyway," Josh said. "You should just walk away from her when she gets like that."

That would have been the logical reaction. But Josh is the one who is logical in our crowd. As for me, well, there was no way I could explain how Addie had reeled me in. She knew exactly what buttons to push to get me to play. That's what years of friendship could do.

"Well, the point is Jenny made the bet, and now we have to help her win," Chloe told Josh. "And besides, I for one would love to see Addie Wilson embarrassed about *her* clothes for once."

I smiled at Chloe. Addie and her pals made fun of Chloe's wardrobe constantly. But Chloe didn't care what they said. Or at least she made it *seem* like she didn't care. I figured somewhere, deep down, being made fun of – for any reason – had to hurt.

Still, Chloe didn't change her style to please the Pops. She did her own thing when it came to clothes. Like today. She was wearing a pair of well-worn jeans, slip-on black-and-white-checked Vans, and a bright orange T-shirt that read: *Help Wanted. Do My Homework.* Not exactly high fashion, but very Chloe.

"It would be great to videotape Addie strolling through the halls in her pajamas," my pal Marc Newman said as he pulled out his ever-present video camera. "Talk about comic relief." Marc was in the middle of filming a documentary about our school. It was going to be sort of like MTV's *The Real World*, except in middle school.

I frowned slightly, considering that. If we didn't come up with a killer booth idea soon, *I'd* be the comic relief. Marc must have seen the look of panic on my face, because he instantly started coming up with ideas for our booth. "We could have a movie trivia booth," he suggested. "You know, you pay money for a chance to answer a question and get a prize."

"You'd be the only one winning anything, *Mr. Spielberg*," Chloe teased him.

"Well, we could make it all kinds of trivia," Marc suggested. "Sports, history, art . . ."

"How about a ring toss booth," my friend Liza suggested. "Or dunk the teacher?"

I shook my head. "None of those are flashy enough," I told Liza and Marc. "We have to do something big. HUGE. Something no one can resist."

Just then, Marilyn and Carolyn, identical twins who hang out with us, sat down at the table. I had to laugh when I saw their lunch trays. They both had placed a milk carton in the upper left corner of the tray, a banana in the lower right corner of the tray, and a tuna hero on a plate in the center. That was Marilyn and Carolyn for you. Even their lunch trays were identical.

"Why don't we have a guess-which-twin-is-which booth?" Josh joked as the girls sat side by side across the table from him.

"*We* can't even always tell that," Marilyn replied, flipping her long blond hair over her shoulder.

"Yeah," Carolyn joked. "Which one am I today?"

I laughed. Sometimes it was really hard for anyone to tell Marilyn and Carolyn apart except themselves. They both had the same long blond hair, small blue eyes, and rosy pudgy cheeks. Luckily, today Marilyn was wearing a skirt and Carolyn was in a pair of khakis.

"Well, whatever we do, count me in to decorate the booth," Liza chimed in. "I'll make it really bright and bold. That will draw people to us right away."

That made me happy. Liza was a really talented artist. She was practically painting all of the sets for our school play, *You're a Good Man, Charlie Brown*, by herself.

"Thanks, Liza," I told her, trying to remain upbeat and enthusiastic. But it was no use. My face fell right back into the frowning position it had been in most of the day. "This is so frustrating," I groaned. "I just know the Pops have come up with something amazing by now. And we don't even have one decent idea for a booth."

"Why don't you just give it up, Jenny?" I spun around and there was Addie.

"So which pajamas are you going to wear? The blue ones with the teddy bears and bows, or the pink flannel ones with the puppies and kittens on them?" Addie continued.

I blushed. My pajamas were cute. But Addie made them sound really babyish. Once again, Addie had used the time we had spent together – this time all of our elementary school sleepovers – to make fun of me. The girl definitely knew too much about me. Luckily, my new friends aren't the kind of people to make fun of someone for the style of pajamas she wears. Instead, they jumped to my defense.

"Oh, she's going to lose, huh?" Marilyn challenged Addie. "Remember the class president election?"

"You were pretty sure you were going to win that, too, weren't you?" Carolyn finished her sister's thought. "But Jenny is your class president, isn't she?"

"That was just a slight glitch in the system," Addie assured the twins. "It won't happen this time. Our booth is going to be a real record breaker."

I sighed. Just as I'd suspected. The Pops already had their idea for a booth. They probably had it half-built by now, too. *Eeergh!*

Before anyone could say anything else, Sabrina Rosen, an eighth grade Pop, walked over to Addie. Behind her were Dana, Claire, and Sam. "Come on, Addie, I need to fix my eyeliner," Sabrina urged, pushing Addie toward the girls' room. The cafeteria bathroom was kind of the Pop clubhouse – the place where they could have fun with their two favorite hobbies: putting on makeup, and putting down anyone who wasn't a Pop.

"Yeah, Addie, come on," Claire urged. "We're off to the loo." She turned and smiled at Sam. "I just love that. The *loo.*"

Sam grinned back at Claire. "This is just like home," she told her. "All the really posh girls in my old school gathered in the loo after lunch, too."

"Posh," Dana repeated, in a very bad imitation of an English accent. She looked at Addie, Sabrina, and Claire. "Did you hear that? We're posh now!"

As the posh Pops walked off, Marc rolled his eyes. "You'd think that was the first time she's ever heard that word," he said.

"Hasn't she heard of Posh Spice from the Spice Girls?" Chloe groaned. "She's Victoria Beckham now. Everyone's heard of *her.*"

I had no idea how much the Pops knew about old school English pop stars who were married to soccer players. In fact, the only thing I knew for sure was that Addie had no intention of losing this bet – especially not to me. And knowing Addie, she would stop at nothing to win.

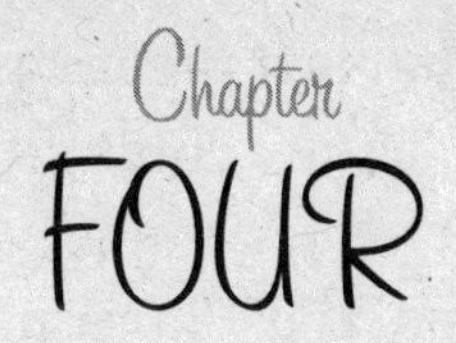

Chapter FOUR

BY THE NEXT MORNING it seemed all of history had changed. I'd always learned that we'd won the Revolutionary War. But this morning it seemed that the British were still running the colonies, *at least at Joyce Kilmer Middle School.*

As I walked down the C wing hall to my locker, I caught a glimpse of Claire and Dana. They were both wearing pencil-tight blue jeans with matching red, white, and blue T-shirts. That wouldn't have seemed very unique, except these shirts didn't have American flag designs on them. Instead, they had the Union Jack – the British flag – splashed across the front.

Claire and Dana were standing by Sam's locker. They were speaking very loudly, just to make sure we could all hear how incredibly English they'd already become.

"I hope they don't have heroes and crisps for lunch again today," Claire mentioned.

That seemed pretty random to me, since it was first thing in the morning, and Claire didn't have lunch until fifth period. But it did give Claire a chance to show off her new British word, which is probably why she brought it up.

"I know," Dana agreed. "The school crisps are so greasy."

Sam laughed. "What is it Americans call crisps again?" she asked. "Oh, yes – potato chips. Which is kind of funny because we call French fries chips."

Immediately, Dana and Claire pulled out their notebooks and began writing. "Chips equals French fries," they murmured as they wrote.

"I'd prefer biscuits," Dana said. "That's cookies, right, Sam?"

As Sam nodded, Dana scribbled something else in her notebook.

"Oh, I don't believe this," Felicia said, coming up beside me. "They're taking notes on everything Sam says."

"You really think that's what they're doing?" I asked her.

"Watch," Felicia urged.

"Let's stop talking about lunch," Sam begged the two Pops. She put her hand on her stomach. "I've got a little bit of a tummy ache. I'm afraid I ate one too many bangers at breakfast."

"Bangers?" Claire asked.

"I think you call them sausages," Sam explained.

"Bangers," Dana and Claire dutifully repeated, writing the word in their notebooks.

Just then, Addie walked down the hall. As usual, she looked really grown-up – almost like a teenager. She was wearing baggy jeans with a few holes in them, and a tight long-sleeved white shirt. Her hair was pulled back into a bun.

"Hi, everyone," Addie greeted Dana, Claire, and Sam. "Like my new jeans?"

Dana and Claire shrugged. "They're okay, but . . ." Claire began.

"Okay?" Addie's voice scaled up a little with surprise. "They're the newest thing. I just got them last night at Oz."

Oz was one of the hottest stores in the mall. If they sold those jeans, they had to be really in fashion.

"Well, they may be the newest thing here," Dana told Addie. "But over in Europe, it's all about tight-leg jeans." She twirled around a little to show Addie what she was wearing. "Sam loaned us these."

"Well, *we* don't live in Europe," Addie reminded her, trying to remain calm, since she knew everyone in the hallway was listening. She wasn't having much luck controlling her temper, though. "We live here. In the United States of America. Not the States, or the colonies, or whatever they call us over there. And trust me. This is what people are wearing here!" And with that, Addie stormed off to her locker, leaving Claire, Dana, and Sam behind.

"I think she's gone a bit *daft*," Claire told Sam, once again using part of her new oh-so-British vocabulary.

"I must admit I don't know why she's got her knickers in such a twist," Sam agreed.

Dana and Claire stared at her.

"I mean, I don't know why she's all upset," Sam

explained, as she watched Dana and Claire write the new expression in their books. "After all, it's just clothes."

I sighed. Obviously, Sam did not know one of the most important unwritten rules of middle school.

MIDDLE SCHOOL RULE #18:

THE PERSON WITH THE HOTTEST CLOTHES LEADS.

That was what was upsetting Addie so much. From the moment she'd entered middle school she'd been the trendsetter – especially when it came to the sixth and seventh grade Pops. Sometimes, even the eighth grade Pops, like Maya and Sabrina, followed her style, which was pretty incredible when you think about it. No one in the school had ever challenged Addie's place as resident fashionista . . . until now.

"This is going to get messy, I can tell," Felicia said.

"Yeah," I agreed.

"Which is a good thing," Felicia continued.

"A good thing?" I repeated, not quite following her.

"Sure," Felicia explained with a grin. "While *they're* battling it out, *we're* going to work as a team to get our booth rolling."

"Well, we have to have a booth first," I reminded her.

"Actually, I have an idea for that," Felicia said. "We could make one of those basketball booths. You know, where people shoot basketballs into baskets that are set at an angle. If they get the ball in, they get a prize. We could have flashing lights that go off when someone gets a basket, just to bring attention to our booth."

Hmmm . . . I had to admit that might work. Basketball booths were always busy at real carnivals. But would it be enough to top the Pops?

"I'll talk to everyone at lunch," I told Felicia.

Felicia nodded. Her eyes looked a little sad though. I knew she felt badly that she and Rachel had fourth period lunch, while the rest of our group of friends ate together in fifth period. Especially because Josh's scheduled lunch period was with us and not her. But we all made a special effort to keep Felicia and Rachel in the loop about what we talked about during lunch. That way they never felt too left out.

"Cool," Felicia said. "Let me know what everyone thinks."

"Will do," I said. "I gotta get to English class now, though."

"Real English class?" Felicia asked with a giggle. She looked over toward where Dana and Claire were once again scribbling ferociously in their notebooks. "Or *Sam's* English class?"

"Cheerio, mates," I joked as I walked down the hall to class.

* * *

By lunchtime, it was clear that the new Pop had taken over.

As I stood in the lunch line, I heard Maya choosing her lunch. "I'll take the green jelly for dessert," she said, pointing to the Jell-O in the cold food line.

"And I'd like a sandwich with no butter beans," Claire added. Considering the only beans on the menu that day were lima, I guessed that butter beans was the English way of saying lima beans.

"I can't believe they don't serve any fizzy drinks in school anymore," Dana sighed, grabbing a bottle of water instead of the soda she really wanted.

"Oh, water's much healthier than a fizzy," Sam pointed out. "Better for your skin. Eight glasses of water a day keeps the spots away."

I figured spots meant pimples.

"I guess," Dana agreed. She smiled at the lunch lady. "I'd like an oatmeal raisin biscuit, too, please."

If the lunch lady was surprised to hear the Pops order in such a weird way, she didn't show it. She just handed Claire her hamburger without a side of lima beans, plopped a bowl of green Jell-O on Maya's tray, and handed Dana her oatmeal raisin cookie without comment.

After Sabrina ordered a "red jelly" for her "sweet" it was Addie's turn to order. "I'll have a hamburger and a carton of milk, please," she told the lunch lady. Then she sighed. "I wish they had some good old American apple pie," she added loudly enough for Sam to hear.

Addie was obviously not taking the Joyce Kilmer Middle School British invasion too well.

But Addie was the only Pop who wasn't totally into it. That became really clear about halfway through lunch, when Chloe came running back all excited from the girls' bathroom. (Chloe is the only person in our school who actually uses the cafeteria girls' room as a bathroom.)

"Boy, do I have news!" Chloe exclaimed, flopping down in her seat.

"What?" Carolyn asked. "Did Sabrina get a new color of eye shadow?"

"No, I bet it's lipstick," Marilyn suggested. "That's bigger news than eye shadow."

Liza giggled. "You guys are so bad," she said. But I could tell she thought the twins were pretty funny.

"No, this is *real* news," Chloe insisted. She turned to me. "You're really going to want to hear this one, Jenny."

"So tell us already," Marc insisted. "I hate when you drag things on and on into infinity."

"Well, technically she can't do that," Josh interrupted. "Because infinity means . . ."

"Chill out, Mr. Mathman," Marc interrupted him. "It's just an expression."

"Come on, Chloe, what did you hear?" I asked, practically begging her to tell us.

Chloe leaned back in her chair and took a deep breath.

I sighed heavily. That was my first clue that she was going to drag this out as long as she could. Once Chloe had everyone's attention, it took her a while to let go of it.

"So I'm in the stall, right?" she began. "And of course the Pops are acting like they don't even know I'm there. But I can hear everything they're saying. They're all standing around, talking in these fake English accents. Except Sam, of course, who really is English so her accent isn't fake but . . ."

"They're all using English accents? You're kidding," Liza interrupted her. She burst out laughing, imagining the Pops trying to echo Sam's accent. "That must have sounded hilarious."

"Hilarious isn't even the word for it," Chloe told her. "You should have heard Dana. Her accent was a cross between a southern accent, an Australian accent, and some weird accent I couldn't identify. I wish I had a tape recorder."

Everyone laughed – everyone but me, that is. I wanted to know what the Pops had said that was so important. "Come on, Chloe," I pleaded. "What's the big news?"

"Right, I'm getting to it," Chloe assured me. "So I'm in the stall, and the Pops start talking about their carnival booth."

Now I was interested. "You know what kind of booth they're having?" I asked, moving to the edge of my seat.

Chloe nodded. "They talked about it, even with me in there. I'm telling you, I felt like some sort of American spy during the Revolution."

"So what kind of booth is it?" Marc asked her.

"A makeover booth," Chloe told us. "The Pops have a great desire to allow us, the unwashed masses, to have a small glimpse into what it takes to be a Pop."

"You mean with their makeup and hairstyles?" Carolyn asked.

Chloe nodded. "And clothes. You get to go into their booth, be made over by one of the Pops, and then have your photo taken as a souvenir."

"So what kind of clothes and makeup are they going to have?" Liza wondered.

"That's the best part," Chloe said. "There was almost a war in there over what fashions they were going to have. Sam volunteered to bring in some of the clothes she'd brought from . . . oh . . . what did she call it? Oh, yeah. *Across the pond.*"

"Figures," Carolyn said.

"Yeah, they're all dressing like her now," Marilyn agreed.

"Not all of them," Chloe told her. "Addie nearly flipped out when she heard Sam's suggestion. I guess she wanted *her* clothes to be the ones in the booth. She told all the Pops that no one in school would want to look like Sam. They'd all want to look like her."

"And that's when you burst into laughter, right?" Marc asked her.

"Almost," Chloe admitted. "I held the giggles in for a few minutes just to hear what would happen next."

"And what did happen next?" Liza asked.

"They held a vote, and Sam's clothes won!" Chloe exclaimed. "It's going to be a British Boutique booth. Can you imagine?"

"How did *Addie* take that?" I wondered.

Chloe grinned. "I got a glimpse of her face as I walked out of the stall and went over to wash my hands. All I can tell you is, if Addie Wilson was a cartoon character, she'd have had real steam coming out of her ears."

Josh shook his head in amazement. "A makeover booth?" he asked in disbelief. "That's the dumbest idea I've ever heard. No boy would ever go near it."

"That makes our basketball booth a slam dunk . . . pun intended," Marc said.

"Exactly," Josh agreed. "You're going to win that bet hands down, Jenny. No one is going to want to go to a Pop makeover booth."

I shook my head. For once, my genius friend was wrong. I knew just how many girls wanted to look and act like a Pop. Even if the boys steered clear, plenty of girls would go to their booth for a chance to be like a Pop – even if it was just for a few minutes and a picture.

Chapter FIVE

BY THE TIME I GOT HOME that afternoon, I was exhausted. I was really stressed out about the carnival. I knew that the idea of a basketball booth was a good one, but I also knew it probably wouldn't be good enough to beat the Pops' British Boutique. Hey, for a minute there, even *I* was thinking it might be fun to get all Popped up for a photo. Which was why as soon as I got into my room, I started looking through my pajama drawer for something that wouldn't be thoroughly embarrassing.

"Well, these are out," I told Cody and Sam as I held up a pair of red-and-white candy-striped pajamas and some fuzzy bunny slippers. When I'd first gotten the pajamas I'd thought they were adorable – Addie had gotten the same ones in green and white and we wore them at a sleepover last Christmas. But, of course, I would be the only one wearing them this time. And there was no way I was wearing fuzzy bunny slippers to school.

"These don't seem too awful," I said, holding up a pink-and-white snowflake-covered thermal top and matching flannel pajama pants. "What do you guys think?"

The mice squeaked at the sound of my voice. Cody moved closer to the bars of his cage and looked around for a treat, which I gave to him, of course. My pets are kind of spoiled, I admit it. But I can't help myself. Cody and Sam have been my best friends since I got them during the summer between fourth and fifth grades.

It was kind of ironic. Unlike my other elementary school best friend, Addie, they would never abandon me. Turns out that while my former best friend had turned into a human rodent and turned on me, these *real* mice were my friends for life!

I sighed. No matter how hard I tried not to admit it, I still missed Addie. My new friends were terrific people, but we didn't have the kind of history that Addie and I did. I missed being around someone who knew me back then.

On the other hand, I still had my memories. And they were pretty good. Even the new rotten Addie couldn't take them away from me. Which led me to add another rule to my ever-growing list of middle school rules no one ever tells you.

MIDDLE SCHOOL RULE #19:

ALWAYS BE YOUR OWN BEST FRIEND. THAT WAY YOU KNOW YOU'VE GOT ONE FRIEND WHO WILL BE LOYAL FOREVER.

So now, as my own official best friend, I had to make a big decision. Was I the kind of friend I wanted to have, or did I want a best friend who was a little cooler? A little funkier? A little more British Pop? Did I need the kind of change the Pops would be offering at their booth?

I shook my head. Even considering going to the Pops' booth at the upcoming carnival made me feel like a traitor to myself. Still, on the other hand . . .

I looked into the mirror that hung beside my desk. The reflection that stared back at me didn't seem like anything special. Same old long, stick-straight brown hair, medium-size green eyes. Not too tall or too small. Not too fat or too thin. Just average.

"What do you guys think?" I asked Sam and Cody, as I studied the pale green polo shirt and jeans I had worn to school that day. "Do I need a makeover?"

Of course, my mice didn't answer me. Or maybe they did. I don't know. I don't really understand squeaks. It's not like I'm Dr. Dolittle or anything. Still, somehow, it was kind of comforting to have *someone* to talk to when I was this bummed out.

But it would have been nice to get an answer to my question. After all, being popular would make people more likely to come to my carnival booth. The question was, did I need a makeover to be popular? Or was I beyond help?

Sometimes even I amaze myself with how much I think about popularity. I really wish I could be more like Chloe, who doesn't particularly care what the Pops say or do. But I'm not Chloe. I do care. And I'm not alone. Most of the kids in my school want to be popular. It's just human nature.

But, of course, my mice aren't human. And they weren't going to give me the answer I needed. In fact, the only place I could think of to find out if I needed a makeover – and if I did, what *kind* of makeover – was on my favorite website, middleschoolsurvival.com.

I went over to my computer and logged on. Then I searched the site until I found just the quiz I was looking for:

Are You a Makeover in the Making?

Are your best friends craving your sense of style? Are you wearing more makeup than a circus clown? Is the closest you've come to lipstick the red lips you get when you drink fruit punch? There's only one way to find out if you need a makeover or a makeunder – take this middleschoolsurvival.com quiz!

1. What color lip gloss did you put on this morning?

A. It's called Chapstick
B. Pale pink or light tan
C. Bright red

That one was easy. I wore Chapstick, same as I did everyday. Sure it was cute and came in a ball on a keychain, but it was Chapstick all the same. I clicked the letter A, and the computer went to the next question.

2. When it comes to blush, what's your style?

A. I use two tones to bring out my cheekbones.

B. I use a little pale pink on my cheeks and blend it in really well.

C. I only blush when I'm embarrassed.

Wow! I didn't even know you could use two blushes at the same time. So option A was definitely out. That meant it was a toss-up between B and C. I'm not usually allowed to wear makeup, except to school dances sometimes. And when I do, my mom makes me rub it in so much, you can hardly tell. On the other hand, I'm a huge blusher. I get embarrassed at just about everything – and there's no hiding it. In the end I clicked the letter B, because I do wear blush (the powder kind) sometimes.

3. How long does it take you to do your hair before school?

A. Ten minutes — I brush it really well and then decide whether to tie it back, wear a headband, put a pretty clip in, or just let it flow naturally.

B. At least 45 minutes — I get up before dawn so I can wash it, blow it dry, and use a hot iron.

C. Less than five minutes — I just run a brush through it and yank it back into a ponytail. No muss, no fuss.

I clicked the letter A for that one. I usually try to make my hair look pretty before school – but there's no way I would ever spend three-quarters of an hour doing it. I would have to get up way too early to do that. I can barely get out of bed on time in the morning as it is.

4. Which best describes your eye style?

A. I usually wear a pale shadow on my lids and then put on a thin layer of mascara. I like to keep things simple.

B. I don't put anything on my eyes. I'm afraid I'll poke myself with a mascara wand!

C. I wear three colors of shadow, some dark liner, and lots of mascara every day.

Letter B for me. All those different colors to choose from seem too complicated to make it worth it.

5. Have you ever been told you dress like a rock singer?

A. Only on Halloween.

B. Sometimes, when I'm all dressed up for a party.

C. Often. In fact, that's the style I'm going for.

Actually, I'd never been told that I looked like a singer or movie star or anything. But it did sort of seem like a great idea for a Halloween costume. So I clicked on the letter A.

6. How do you choose your outfit for school?

A. I spend the hour before bed trying on different looks in front of the mirror.

B. If it's clean and on the top of the pile when I wake up, I throw it on.

C. I have my favorite looks, and I can pretty much put them together in a few minutes.

For me, that answer was C. I really like wearing jeans and a top – especially long-sleeved solid T-shirts, or colorful polo shirts with collars. I like to be comfortable, but I also like to be neat. And I stick to purples, blues, and greens a lot in my shirts – I think I look best in those colors. In fact, most of my wardrobe is made up of blue jeans, green shirts, and purple shirts. So it's pretty hard to go wrong.

7. How much jewelry do you usually wear?

A. I never wear any jewelry to school. Bracelets and rings are distracting and I always wind up playing with my necklaces.

B. I keep it simple. One small necklace or a single bracelet and that's it.

C. Bring on the bling. Rings, bracelets, necklaces, hoop earrings. I like to shimmer when I walk down the hall.

I fingered the small silver butterfly charm that I was wearing on a chain around my neck. It was really pretty, but also very simple. That was how I liked things. Letter B for me.

That was the last question on the quiz. A moment later, the computer began totaling my points.

So, are you ready for a makeover or a make*under?* Check the chart below to see whether you need to pump up the volume or totally turn it down when it comes to your makeup routine.

1.	A. 1 point	B. 2 points	C. 3 points
2.	A. 3 points	B. 2 points	C. 1 point
3.	A. 2 points	B. 3 points	C. 1 point
4.	A. 2 points	B. 1 point	C. 3 points
5.	A. 1 point	B. 2 points	C. 3 points
6.	A. 3 points	B. 1 point	C. 2 points
7.	A. 1 point	B. 2 points	C. 3 points

After adding up my answers, the computer told me I had eleven points. But what did that mean?

16–21 points: Aaaaah! There's a product explosion in your makeup bag. Hide the tweezers, ban the blow-dryer, and leave the ruby red lips to Snow White. And as for all that bling — you've got to tone it down, girl. Stop hiding behind a mask of makeup — get a more natural look and let the real you shine through!

10–15 points: This is the look you're aiming for. You're not too wild, but you're not all granola and natural, either. You've managed to balance yourself on that tightrope between done up and just plain overdone. Congrats!

7–9 points: You've taken the natural look to an extreme. There are a lot of reasons you could be barefaced and beautiful. Maybe you're just not into all that girly stuff. Or maybe you just love yourself the way you are — no improvements necessary. If that's you, stick to your guns. There's nothing more beautiful than a gal with self-confidence. However, if the truth is you're curious about makeup and hair products, but you're confused about how to use them, don't be afraid to ask a stylish friend or someone who works at a makeup counter at the mall for a few free tips. You may be surprised at what a change just a few dabs of blush and lip gloss can make — not a brand-new you, just a fresher version of your already wonderful self.

I thought about my results for a few minutes. Ten points. That meant I was just on the border of having found a nice makeover middle ground and being in need of a makeover. I was safe, but just by a hair. Long, straight, *boring* hair.

Somehow, I didn't find that too comforting. I thought about what the website had said about asking for makeup advice from a friend whose style you admired. A little advice from Sam probably wouldn't do me any harm. Not that she was my friend or anything, but she was someone whose taste in clothing seemed a little daring and undeniably cool. That was exactly what I wanted to be. And I wondered just how many kids in my school were thinking the exact same thing. I sighed heavily as I caught a glimpse of the pile of pajamas lying on my floor. Probably plenty. And they'd all be at the Pops' British Boutique on the day of the carnival.

Chapter SIX

AS FELICIA AND I GOT OFF the bus at school the next morning, I heard music playing in the parking lot. *Loud* music. I'd never heard the song before. It was kind of a mix of pop music and dance music. That was perfect, because whatever song it was, it was making *our* Pops dance.

"What's going on?" I asked, walking over to where Marc was standing, his video camera in hand.

"I'm calling it Blacktop Disco," Marc told Felicia and me. "At least that's my working title."

We all watched as Sabrina and Claire turned and tried to bump rear ends. Only they wound up missing and . . . *boom.* Claire fell to the ground. Marc tried to hold his camera steady as he laughed.

"That had to hurt," Felicia said.

The Pops' impromptu dance performance was not going unnoticed. The rest of the student body all seemed to be standing around staring at them as they moved. That would have been horrifying to me – I was blushing just thinking about it. But the Pops were so used to being the center of attention that it was just another day for them.

As I looked around, I spotted someone in the crowd of

non-dancing kids who surprised me. Usually, Addie would be right out there in the midst of things – flailing her arms and leaping up and down like a pogo stick with the other Pops. But today, she was standing over by the wall, all by herself, checking out her makeup in a compact mirror. She seemed to be making a big point of not being interested in what Maya, Claire, Sabrina, and Dana were doing.

Just then, Chloe came running over to us, dragging Liza by the arm. "Hey, guys, wait until you see what Liza did last night," she said as she reached us. "It's amazing."

To me, it was even more amazing that Chloe seemed oblivious to the dancing spectacle in the middle of the parking lot. But maybe she had the right idea. The less attention paid to the Pops, the better. I turned to Liza. "What did you do?" I asked her.

Liza blinked for a minute, as if trying to refocus her attention from the spectacle in front of us. "Oh, I drew this," she said, pulling out her sketchbook and opening it to a brightly colored page.

"Wow! This is incredible!" I exclaimed, looking at the drawing in front of me. It was a picture of a basketball booth at a carnival, and it was awesome.

"I thought we could take pictures of basketball players from the Internet, and have them blown up to life-size," Liza said, pointing to some sketches of very tall men that she had placed on the sides of the booth in her drawing. "It wouldn't cost much. And it would be a lot of fun for people to see how they measure up to the real NBA players."

"Exactly," Chloe agreed. "It would give them something to do while they're waiting in line for their turn."

I smiled. "Waiting in line?" I repeated. "You're being optimistic."

"I predict long lines," Chloe told me.

"Predict, huh?" I said. "Maybe we should have a fortune-telling booth instead. Madame Chloe reads the future."

Chloe shook her head. "No thanks. I'm no fortune-teller. Even I couldn't have predicted *that.*" She pointed to where the Pops were dancing.

"I think it looks like fun," Liza told Chloe. "Only I would never have the guts to dance like that out here."

"I kind of figured Addie would be right in the middle of all this," Felicia said. "She's never afraid to be the center of attention."

I glanced over toward the far wall where Addie stood. Boy did she look angry. Her blue eyes were squeezed tight into little slits, and her lips were pierced tightly. It was the kind of look she usually reserved for me when I did something she didn't like. But today, her anger was all aimed at the Pops in general – and at Sam in particular.

I sure wouldn't want to be Sam right now. She might be the Pop Queen from England today, but her rule wasn't going to last. I'd seen what Addie could be like when she felt angry or threatened. It wasn't pretty.

"So, do you like the drawing?" Liza asked hopefully, interrupting my thoughts.

"It's amazing," I assured her. "*You're* amazing. But . . ."

"But you're worried that it isn't going to be enough to keep you out of pajamas," Liza said.

I nodded. "Look around. Half the people here are trying to do the same dance the Pops are. And that's out here in the parking lot. Imagine if they get to actually dress like a Pop at the carnival and have photographic proof of how cool they look."

"The Pops don't look so cool," Chloe assured me. She pointed to the tangled mass of arms and legs in the dance circle.

"Neither will I in my pajamas," I said.

"So who cares?" Chloe answered. "I think wearing pajamas to school could be fun. They're comfortable and relaxing. In fact, you know what? If you wind up wearing pajamas to school, I will, too."

"Me, too," Felicia agreed.

"We could get the twins to wear matching robes," Chloe suggested.

"A school pajama party," Liza added. "I like it."

I grinned. "You guys better watch out. Marc's got all of this on videotape. I just might hold you to it."

"You won't have to," Chloe said. "We're going to win."

I smiled at her. I was so lucky. I had the best friends in the world. They were totally willing to embarrass themselves in front of everyone, just so I wouldn't have to be embarrassed alone.

I felt better about the whole pajama drama. I was

actually looking forward to the carnival. Let the Pops do their worst. There was nothing they could do to hurt me now. There was power in friendship. Real friendship. Not the I'm-your-friend-as-long-as-you-wear-the-right-clothes-and-do-the-right-dances kind of friendships the Pops had.

Suddenly, a strange feeling came over me. *I actually felt sorry for Addie Wilson.* After all, she and I had once had a real friendship, like the kind I had with my new friends. But Addie didn't have that in her life anymore. She was all alone. I wondered how long she'd be able to stand it.

Apparently, not very long at all. That afternoon, when all the other Pops went into the bathroom for their regular lunchtime gloss and gossip fest, Addie came over to our table instead.

"Hey, Jenny, can I talk to you for a minute?" she asked me.

"Are you giving up on the bet?" Marilyn asked her.

"You may as well, you're going to lose anyway," Carolyn added.

Addie rolled her eyes. "I don't know why you people are so obsessed with that bet," she said, trying to sound all bored and superior. "There are much more important things going on around here."

"You mean like the sudden rise of Sam?" Chloe asked her.

I almost thought I heard Addie gasp, like the wind had

been knocked out of her. But when I looked at her a moment later, she was back to her cool, calm, collected Pop self. Obviously, there was no way she was going to let anyone – least of all me – see that Chloe had hit a nerve.

"Actually, I was referring to student council business," Addie told Chloe. She turned to me: "You know, it's going to be the sixth grade's turn to sell school T-shirts and pennants at the soccer game in a few weeks, and I thought we should meet to discuss how we're going to do it."

I was confused. She wanted to talk about how we were going to sell T-shirts? There was nothing to it. Every grade sold them the same way. Either Addie or I would send out an e-mail asking for volunteers. Then, on the morning of the game, we'd sell the T-shirts for ten dollars each. No big deal. Certainly not big enough to require a meeting between Addie and me.

"Jenny, I think we should really put a little effort into this," Addie insisted, before I could utter a word. "We have to show the upper grades that we can handle the responsibility. And we've never actually done this before. Better to be overprepared, right?"

I sighed. When she put it that way, there was no arguing.

Addie smiled triumphantly as she studied the look on my face. "Good. We'll meet at my house after school. You'll just get off the bus at my stop."

"No," I told her firmly.

The kids at my table all stared at me. They were shocked at my new ability to defy Addie's wishes.

"I have to drop some things off at my house first," I added.

Out of the corner of my eye I could see Chloe and the twins shaking their heads in disapproval.

"Fine," Addie said. "I'll see you later." Then, before I could change my mind, she walked off toward the girls' room.

"I can't believe you agreed to go to her house," Chloe said to me.

I shrugged. "Well, it *is* a student council thing, and I *am* the sixth grade president."

"You could have met at school," Chloe replied.

"I know," I agreed. "But she's Addie." I didn't think any other explanation was necessary.

"She sure is a force of nature," Liza agreed.

"Yeah, but so is a tornado," Marc pointed out.

"Tornadoes cause less destruction than Addie Wilson," Josh said.

"You're not kidding," Chloe agreed. "Addie is dangerous."

"Watch out for her," Carolyn warned me.

"I think she's up to something," Marilyn seconded.

I nodded. "Don't worry," I assured my friends. "I think she's just trying to show off to the upper grades. And that helps all of us."

"If you say so," Chloe replied with a shrug. "But don't say we didn't warn you."

"And don't agree to any more bets," Liza said.

"You don't have to worry about that," I assured her. "I've definitely learned my lesson."

"Just remember, Addie likes the element of surprise," Josh reminded me.

I smiled. "The only way Addie Wilson could surprise me is if she didn't try to surprise me," I told him confidently.

Chapter SEVEN

WHICH MEANT THAT I WASN'T surprised at all.

Sure enough, Addie did have something unexpected waiting for me when I arrived at her house that afternoon. Samantha was there, too. She was sitting on Addie's floor, checking out her CD collection.

"Hi, Jenny," Sam greeted me as I walked into the room.

"Um . . . hi . . ." I said, looking at her curiously. "I . . . uh . . . I didn't know you were . . ."

"I thought it would be a good idea to get Sam involved right away with our class," Addie said sweetly. "She'll feel less like the new girl that way."

Sam smiled gratefully at Addie. "We sold T-shirts at our school football games at home, and it was such fun." She stopped and looked at Addie and me. "I mean *soccer* games," she corrected herself.

"We know football means soccer in England," Addie said, sounding slightly annoyed. Then she smiled and quickly changed her tone. "Do you see any music you want to listen to?" she asked.

Sam shrugged. "I don't really know a lot of these groups," she admitted. "I'll leave it up to you."

Addie grinned so widely, I thought her face might tear

in half. Obviously, those were words she'd been dying to hear Sam say for a long time. "Okay," Addie told her as she picked a CD out of the pile. "This one's awesome."

"So you're student council president," Sam told me. "That's absolutely brilliant."

"She means awesome," Addie told me. Then she turned to Sam. "Jen's only president of the *sixth grade*, not the whole student council."

"And Addie's *vice* president of the sixth grade," I added, just to set the record straight.

"We work so well together," Addie said, not taking my bait. "In fact, Jenny and I have a little competition going to see whose booth can make the most money at the carnival."

"That's not working together," Sam pointed out. "That's working against each other."

"Not really," Addie insisted.

Sam looked at her curiously. So did I. I was dying to see how Addie could possibly turn our bet into a team effort.

"The bet is making us both work really hard to make the best booths at the carnival. And the more money we raise, the more the sixth grade can donate to the earthquake victims in South America."

I stared at Addie, amazed. She'd done it. Up until now, she'd been so mean about the bet. But the way she was describing it now, it seemed like a great idea. Just a friendly bet, benefiting the people who needed the money most. I had to admit it, Addie really was something else. There was no one like her.

Apparently, Samantha thought so, too. "Oh, that's brill, Addie," she said. "You're quite clever."

"So I've been told," Addie replied.

"And she's modest, too," I mumbled under my breath.

"What?" Addie asked me.

"Oh, um, nothing," I said. "I just think we should plan things out for the T-shirt sale. I need to get home. I didn't get a chance to feed Cody and Sam."

"Her *mice.*" Addie made a face as she explained who Cody and Sam were.

"Ooh, your mouse has the same name as I do," Sam said. She actually sounded pleased about it. I relaxed a little. Maybe Sam wasn't so bad after all.

"I had a ferret back home in England," Sam continued. "Her name was Francine."

"Francine Ferret," I repeated. "I like that."

Sam sighed. "I miss Francine," she said. "You know, people always freak out when they hear you have a ferret for a pet. But they can actually give you a lot of love."

"I know," I agreed. "Sam and Cody are so soft and cuddly. They're not at all like people think mice might be."

"I'd love to meet them someday," Sam told me. "Maybe feed them a treat or something."

Addie looked at us both strangely. Then she pulled a big black case out of her closet. "You guys want to do makeovers?" she asked, changing the subject from ferrets and mice to something she was more comfortable with.

"Sure," Sam agreed.

"I really should get going," I said slowly. "If we could just decide who will make the T-shirt stand sign-up sheet, then . . ."

"Oh, come on, Jenny," Addie urged me. "All work and no play is no fun. Stay for a while and try on some of this stuff. You can't just run off – you haven't been over here in ages."

And whose fault is that? I thought. But I didn't say that. I just couldn't. There was a part of me that was so flattered by being welcomed back into Addie's life that I didn't want to do anything to spoil it. Especially since I knew it wasn't going to last.

"You know what?" Addie said, pulling out some green eye shadow. "I'm bored with regular old makeovers. I already know how to put my makeup on perfectly."

I rolled my eyes, but again, I kept my mouth shut.

"Let's do something more fun," Addie suggested. She reached into her closet and pulled out a bunch of old picture books. "Let's make ourselves up to look like the characters in these books."

I looked at her strangely. "Why?" I asked her.

"Because it will be fun," Addie insisted. "Something different to do."

Sam held up a book about snakes. "I love the colors on this snake's skin. Maybe I can repeat the pattern on my cheek." She picked out some black eyeliner, and yellow and orange eye shadow.

"Oh, I want to look like this little rag doll," Addie squealed, holding up a well-worn picture book with a toy chest on the cover. "This was my favorite book when I was little." She picked up a red lipstick and began coloring a circle on the tip of her nose.

I watched as Samantha drew an intricate pattern of squares and diamonds around one of her eyes and down the side of her cheek with black eyeliner and then began coloring them in with the shadows. It did look snake-like – and kind of pretty.

"Come on, Jenny," Sam urged. "You didn't just come round to talk a few minutes and leave."

Actually I *had* just "come round" for that. But I didn't want to seem like the party pooper here – especially around Addie, the party queen. Besides, it did look as though they were having a good time.

"Here, try this one," Addie said, pulling an encyclopedia of dogs out of her closet. Ever since I can remember, Addie has been trying to get her parents to buy her a puppy. But so far, the Wilsons are completely dogless.

I opened the book and flipped through the pages. My eyes finally landed on a black-and-white bulldog who had this black circle around his eye. He was *so* adorable. Without a second thought, I picked up a black eyeliner and began to draw a crooked circle around one of my eyes.

"You look fab," Sam remarked admiringly.

"Adorable, Jen," Addie cooed.

"You look really cute, too," I told Addie, as I checked out the freckles she'd dotted on her cheeks, and the triangle shapes she'd drawn around her eyes with black eyeliner. "Like Raggedy Ann, except with blond hair. This is so much more fun than just a regular old makeover. Those are boring."

The minute the words came out of my mouth I regretted them. I hadn't been trying to put down the Pops' idea of a fun carnival booth. But that was pretty much what I'd done. I sat back and braced myself for Addie's furor.

But if Addie had noticed what I'd said, she didn't let on. She just grinned and put some red lipstick circles on her cheeks. Then she looked over at Sam's makeup creation. "Wow, check you out," she said. "That's gorgeous."

"It looks like a painting," I agreed, studying Sam's orange, yellow, and black cheek. "I'm blown away."

"Blown away?" Sam asked.

"Amazed," Addie told her. She sounded very pleased to be translating a word for Sam for a change. "In a good way."

"Oh. We say gobsmacked back home," Sam said.

"Gobsmacked," I repeated. Then I laughed. It was a funny-sounding word.

Addie reached into her backpack and smiled as she pulled out her cell phone. "Come on, we have to take pictures," she said. "That design on your face is too gorgeous not to be remembered. And Jen, you look just like a dog . . ."

She stopped, realizing that now *she* had said something wrong. "In a cute way, I mean," she added.

I grinned. "Arf. Arf," I barked.

"Okay you guys, now get in close," Addie said, opening her phone and pressing the camera button.

"Now let me get one of you and Sam," I said, reaching for Addie's phone. My cell phone doesn't have a camera on it. Addie grinned and went to sit beside Sam. I snapped a picture of the two of them together.

"Now one of Sam alone," Addie said. "Her design really is the most incredible."

I had to agree. So I snapped a beautiful photo of the side of Sam's face. "You'll e-mail these to me, right?" I asked Addie. "I want copies."

"I'd love some as well," Sam said.

"Oh, I promise to e-mail these photos as soon as you guys go home," Addie assured us.

"Speaking of which," I said, looking down at my watch. "I've got to get going. My mom is going to be really angry if I'm late." I stood up and walked over toward the bathroom. "I'm going to wash this off first though. I don't want to run into anyone on the street when I look like a bulldog. How embarrassing would that be?"

Addie giggled. "Totally. Use the cold cream under the sink. That will get the makeup off really fast."

"I'm going to call my mum and have her pick me up," Sam said as I headed toward the door. "Do you want a ride home, Jen?"

I shook my head. "I live really close. I'm going to walk."

"Oh, okay," Sam said. She studied her face in Addie's mirror. "You know, I'm going to leave this on for a while. I want my mum to see it."

Addie grinned happily. "I'll bet you wish everyone could see it."

"I think it's kind of interesting," Sam admitted. "I know my mates at home would love it."

"If you wore that to school in England, your *mates* would be gobsmacked," I said.

Sam laughed. "Maybe not," she said. "My mates over there are really adventurous."

I waited for Addie to get angry at the suggestion that she wasn't adventurous, too. But she didn't. In fact, Addie seemed to just shrug it off. "I guess we seem pretty tame to you," was all she said.

"Not tame," Sam answered. "Just a little afraid to be different. Maybe more predictable."

Uh-oh. Addie wasn't going to like that one bit.

Or was she? Maybe the Pop Addie would have gotten upset at a comment like that. But this new Addie – or maybe she was more like the *old* Addie – didn't seem to be insulted. "Wait until you live here for a while," was all she said. "You'll see we're full of surprises, too."

I had just gotten home when my cell phone began to ring. I looked at the flashing name. Oh good. Chloe. I couldn't wait to tell her that everything with Addie had gone really well.

Fab even. I figured she'd be absolutely gobsmacked when I told her that Addie hadn't been up to anything after all. She'd just wanted to have some fun with an old friend and a new one. Maybe things were changing.

"Hey, Chloe," I said as I answered the phone. "You won't believe what happened at Addie's today. We . . ."

"Uh, Jen . . ." Chloe interrupted me.

But I wasn't going to let her change the subject until I got to talk. This was too important. "Addie didn't have an ulterior motive or anything," I said excitedly. "In fact, she was really nice. I think she's sick of all this fighting and . . ."

"Jen . . ." Chloe repeated. "You need to know something."

"No, wait," I said. "We actually had fun over there. You won't believe what we did."

"Face painting," Chloe replied.

Huh? "How did you know that?"

"*Everybody* knows it," Chloe answered.

"What are you talking about?"

Chloe sighed. "Are you near your computer?"

"Yeah."

"Turn it on. Check your e-mail."

I did as I was told. And a moment later, I was staring at a huge picture of Sam and myself in our snake and dog modes.

The message in the subject line of the e-mail read: A MAJOR FASHION DON'T.

Then, under the picture, Addie had typed: *This is Sam's idea of a makeover . . . don't let her* take-*over!*

Addie hadn't lied to Sam. She sure was full of surprises. *Rotten* surprises. The e-mail had been sent to the entire sixth grade – not to mention Pops in the seventh and eighth grades as well.

"But Addie was wearing weird makeup, too. She looked like a rag doll – with a red nose and freckles and . . ." I stammered, unable to stop staring at the picture of myself on the computer screen.

"Yeah, well, she conveniently left those pictures out of the e-mail," Chloe said.

"She's probably erased them by now," I moaned.

"Gotten rid of the evidence," Chloe agreed.

"I can't believe this," I murmured, shaking my head. "She seemed so nice. And I thought she really was starting to like Sam, too."

"Oh I'm sure this whole thing was about Sam," Chloe told me. "She just wanted to embarrass her in front of the Pops. They're not going to be too impressed with her now. Somehow I can't see any of them coming to school with their faces painted."

"But why did she do this to me?" I wondered out loud, even though I already knew the answer. Simple. She hated me.

"She's still mad that you're the class president," Chloe said. "And besides, showing Sam hanging out with one of us is the ultimate way of getting her out of the Pops.

You know the Pops never hang out with anyone except themselves."

"But Addie was hanging out with us all afternoon," I insisted.

"Yeah, but she doesn't say that in the e-mail," Chloe pointed out. "For all anyone knows, she just saw you hanging out on the street made up like this."

"And she makes it seem like it's something Sam thinks is stylish. That's not it at all," I complained.

"Gee, Addie exaggerated to get her way," Chloe remarked sarcastically. "Like *that* never happened before."

I sighed. I couldn't believe I had been fooled by Addie . . . again. When was I ever going to learn? Addie and I weren't friends anymore. And we never would be.

"There is *one* good thing about all this," Chloe pointed out.

I sighed. Even someone as optimistic as Chloe could never put a positive spin on something this awful. "What could possibly be good about it?" I demanded.

"Well," Chloe said, trying to sound cheerful. "Walking around school in pajamas won't seem so embarrassing after this."

All I could do was groan. I mean, what else was there to say?

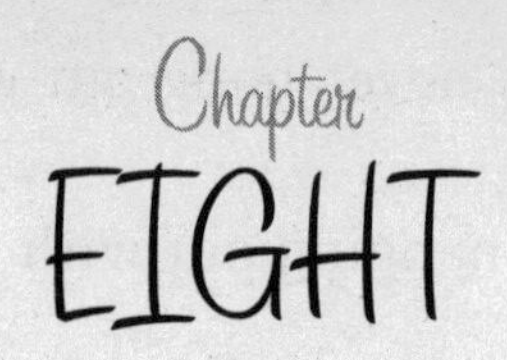

Chapter EIGHT

SAM WAS SITTING ALL BY HERSELF at lunch the next day. I stared at her for a moment, amazed. No, I wasn't surprised Addie had managed to ostracize the new girl from the Pops. I knew those photos would definitely do the trick. What I found incredible was how calm and confident Sam seemed as she sat at a table with no one else around. If that had been me . . .

Wait. It *had* been me. On the first day of school, Addie had totally rejected me, leaving me with no one to sit with at lunch. I'd eaten lunch in the phone booth so no one could see what a loser I was.

But Sam wasn't hiding from anyone. She was sitting there, seemingly happy as a clam, peeling her orange. Still, I had a feeling her confident grin was all for effect. It had to hurt her to be the new object of the Pops' ridicule. My friends and I all knew how that felt. Which was probably why I stopped in my tracks when I got to Sam. "Hey, do you want to have lunch with us?" I asked her, pointing to my table of friends.

Sam looked up at me, surprised. "Me?"

I glanced at all the empty chairs around her and

shrugged. Sam giggled. "I guess you couldn't be talking to anyone else, huh?" she said.

I shook my head. "Come on. You'll like my friends. They're a lot of fun."

"Wow. Thanks. Sure. That would be nice," Sam said, picking up her tray and following me over to the table I usually shared with my friends.

If Sam had looked surprised when I'd stopped to invite her to sit with us at lunch, it was nothing compared to the expressions on my friends' faces when she reached our table. It's not often that a Pop – or even a former Pop – comes to sit with us.

But my friends aren't snobs. They wouldn't hold it against someone just because they had once been drawn to the dark side. So Liza moved over and made room for Sam and me at the table. For a moment, nobody said anything. They just sat there. Silent. Which was really weird for us. But I guess my friends weren't sure whether or not to trust Sam. Not that I blamed them. Up until the photo incident, Sam hadn't exactly been overly friendly to us. Not that we'd gone out of our way to make her feel welcome, either.

"So, Chloe, how's your solo going?" I asked, trying to get the conversation started again.

"It's okay," she said. "It's just a few lines."

"Chloe's in the school's fall musical," I explained to Sam. "We're doing *You're a Good Man, Charlie Brown.*"

"Oh, that's fab," Sam said. "What part do you have?"

I flinched slightly. That was a bad question to ask. The fact that Chloe hadn't gotten the part of Lucy, and was only in the chorus, was still a sore spot with her.

"I'm just one of the people in the chorus," Chloe said, taking a bite out of her sandwich.

"She's the understudy to the girl playing Lucy, too," Liza pointed out. "And she's got a solo in one of the songs."

"It's not a big solo," Chloe corrected her.

"Come on, Chloe. You know what they say," Marilyn told her. "There are no small parts . . ."

"Only small actors," Carolyn finished her sister's thought.

Sam looked at the twins in surprise.

"They're always doing things like that," Josh told her.

"It's a twin thing," Marilyn and Carolyn said in unison. We all broke into giggles at their timing.

And then, everything went all quiet again. It was like no one was sure what to say with Sam around. Finally, it was Chloe who said what everyone was thinking. "So, are you still friends with them?" she asked.

I gasped. "Chloe . . ." I began.

"What?" Chloe asked. "It's not like that's not what we were all thinking."

I guess Marc could feel some dramatic tension stirring because he pulled out his video camera and began panning around the table. Sam stared at him curiously. "It's for a documentary I'm making," he explained to Sam.

"So? Are you?" Chloe repeated.

Sam glanced over toward the Pops' table. But her expression wasn't one of longing or anything. It was more like a look of disgust. "No. I was never friends with them. Not really. Frankly, I don't think they could be friends with anyone."

"Other than themselves, you mean," I pointed out.

Sam shook her head. "No, I mean with anyone. They only think about themselves. They'd turn on one another in an instant."

"Oh, they have," Marilyn and Carolyn said in unison.

"You should have seen them when Addie wrote the gossip column in the school newspaper. They were fighting with one another all the time," Liza explained.

"But they always seem to find their way back to one another," Chloe pointed out, eyeing Sam carefully.

"Well, don't worry. I'm not like them," she assured Chloe. "In fact, to prove it, why don't I help you with your carnival booth?"

Now Chloe seemed *really* distrustful. "Yeah right. Like we're going to fall for that."

I sighed. *Here we go again*, I thought. Chloe could be so paranoid. Like the time she thought Josh was spying for the Pops during my sixth grade president campaign. Of course, he wasn't. But Chloe sure was convinced he was. I had no intention of going through that all over again. “How would you want to help?” I asked Sam.

“Well, I have an idea that I think could really blow their makeover booth out of the water,” she said slowly.

Something in her tone got me really excited. But Chloe didn’t seem to share my feeling. “We already have an idea for a booth,” she told Sam. “A hoop-shooting contest. That’s basketball,” she added.

Sam nodded. “I know,” she said sweetly. “And that’s a great idea. But maybe we could combine the basketball and my idea. You know, a double-purpose booth. I’m telling you, we made gobs of money with the booth we had at our school carnival back home.”

So Sam had planned a carnival booth before. She had experience – that put us one step ahead of the Pops. And better yet, her booth had made “gobs of money.” That was something that got *everyone’s* attention. “What kind of booth was it?” I asked her excitedly.

Sam looked around the room. I followed her glance. The Pops were nearing our table on their way to the girls’ room.

“Here comes the loo troop,” Sam said, rolling her eyes. “Best to talk about this somewhere more private.”

I nodded. “Good idea,” I agreed. Then I smiled at my friends. “How about we meet at my house after school today? You can tell us your idea then.”

“I’m free,” Liza said.

“Me, too,” Marc agreed.

"No mathletes' meeting today. So I can come," Josh said. He paused. "Does Felicia have basketball practice this afternoon?"

I grinned at him. "I don't think so. And I'm pretty sure she'll want to be part of this meeting – especially since the basketball thing was her idea."

The smile on Josh's face when he heard Felicia would be there was hilarious. He was obviously soooo crazy about her. Everyone could tell, even Sam, who barely knew either of them. Josh blushed as he noticed us all trying not to laugh at his expression.

"I'll ask Rachel, too," I said, changing the topic slightly to spare Josh any more embarrassment. "And we've got plenty of good snacks."

"Excellent," Marc said, putting away his camera. "There's no sense having a meeting without eating."

"So now tell us," I begged Sam later that afternoon as my friends and I gathered in my kitchen. "What kind of booth did you have at your school carnival that made you so much money?" I was practically bursting at the seams, I was so curious!

"It was a food booth," Sam explained. "We sold fish and chips. Everyone gets hungry at a carnival. We made a fortune!"

"Hey, I thought we'd already agreed on having a basketball booth," Felicia said, suddenly becoming fiercely protective of her idea.

"We are," Sam assured her. "But as I was telling your mates at lunch, maybe we could combine the two ideas." She turned to me. "Has anyone else volunteered to sell food in their booth?"

I shook my head. "No. It's just games – and makeovers."

"Selling food is a great idea," Josh piped up. Then he noticed the scowl on Felicia's face. "As long as we have a basketball game there, too, I mean."

"Of course," Sam assured him. "People can buy food to eat while they're waiting in the queue to play basketball. We can call it The Sports Café."

"The Sports Café! That's a terrific idea!" I exclaimed.

"Oh yeah!" Marc agreed. "It's a guaranteed hit."

"I think so, too," Felicia agreed.

I smiled. Now that Felicia had agreed to add Sam's idea to hers, we had the sign of approval we needed. "Let's celebrate with some s'mores," I said as I went to the cupboard and pulled out the marshmallows, chocolate bars, and graham crackers. Immediately we all began piling the chocolate and marshmallows onto the crackers.

"What do you call these again?" Sam asked.

"S'mores," Chloe told her.

"They look really delicious," Sam said.

"Wait until we put them in the oven so the marshmallow and chocolate melt," Marc told Sam as he placed his s'more on the cookie sheet my mother had left on the counter for us.

"Mmm . . ." Josh licked his lips. "I think the first time I

ever had a s'more was at summer camp. It was the only edible food I had all summer."

"You're really supposed to cook the marshmallows over a campfire," Carolyn explained to Sam.

"But an oven's almost as good," Marilyn countered.

"Agreed," Carolyn told her sister with a smile.

"I can't wait to try one," Sam said eagerly. She placed her s'more on the baking sheet and watched as my mom put a batch of s'mores in the oven. "Maybe we should sell *these* at The Sports Café. Sweets would be an even bigger hit than fish and chips, don't you think?"

I nodded. "Totally."

"Okay, the first batch is done," my mother interrupted us cheerfully as she brought a plate of baked s'mores to the table. "Careful, though. They're hot."

"Thanks, Mrs. McAfee," Chloe said, grabbing a graham cracker, chocolate, and marshmallow sandwich from the plate.

"This is what I was hoping for when my mum and dad told me we were moving to the States," Sam said.

"What was?" I asked.

"I wanted a real American experience," Sam explained. "I wanted to do things the way you do them. But when I was hanging around with Addie and her lot, I didn't think I was going to get the chance."

"Why?" Felicia asked. "The Pops are American, too."

"The Pops?" Sam asked me.

"As in *Pop*-ular," I explained to her.

"That's quite clever," Sam said with a laugh. "The thing is, the *Pops* didn't seem to want to do anything American when I was around. They kept trying to act like they were from the U.K."

She was right. In my mind, I kept picturing Claire and Dana following Sam around with their little notebooks, copying down every word she said. The image made me laugh out loud.

I looked around the room. Everyone seemed really relaxed and happy. Nobody was giving me dirty looks because my mom was there. The Pops would make fun of anyone who spent more than three minutes with their parents when their friends were around. Which just goes to show how nice my new friends really are. They don't even mind when you have a parental unit in the room. (Of course, it didn't hurt that my mom was carrying a plate of hot and tasty s'mores.)

"Mmm . . ." Sam purred as she took her very first bite of a s'more. "This is heaven."

"I know," Rachel agreed, wiping a string of dripping marshmallow from her chin. "I can't ever eat enough of these. Say, did you guys hear the one about the graham cracker who . . ."

"No! Please, no!" Felicia said, jokingly falling to her knees and begging Rachel to stop. "No jokes."

Rachel giggled. "Okay, I'll let you off easy this time."

"We should get back to planning our booth," I said,

changing the subject before Rachel could change her mind about the joke.

"We can't just sell s'mores at the café," Liza pointed out. "What else can we make?"

"I don't know," Sam replied. "What kinds of foods do American kids like?"

"I'll bet pretty much the same foods you do," I said. Then I wiped off my hands and headed for the computer. "I'll check middleschoolsurvival.com for recipes."

Once again, my all-time fave website did not disappoint. "Ooh, look! Caramel apples!" Rachel shouted as she peered over my shoulder. "Those are my favorite!"

"I'm so glad I got my braces off in time for the carnival," Felicia said. "I'll just take out my retainer, and I can eat as many caramel apples as I want."

"Until you get a stomachache," I pointed out. "Those things are really sweet."

"And really good," Liza added. She picked up a pencil and began sketching on a napkin. In just a few seconds she'd come up with a really cool sign. It had a sketch of a caramel apple on a stick. Above the apple she'd written: Gooey Good Caramel Apples: $1.

"That's really good," Sam complimented her. "How did you think that up so quickly?"

Liza shrugged. "It just came to me."

"Liza's an incredible artist," Chloe told Sam. "She's designing the booth for us."

"Excellent," Sam replied.

"Hey, do you guys know why the apple went out with the fig?" Rachel piped up. "Because he couldn't find a date. Get it? A date?"

"We got it," Marc said, rolling his eyes. "And we're giving it back."

"I thought it was funny," Sam said.

Chloe grinned. "That's because you're new to Rachel's jokes. Don't worry. In a few weeks you'll think they're as bad as we do."

"Thanks a lot," Rachel said. But she didn't sound angry. She knew we were just teasing.

"Now, about that recipe," Liza said, bringing us all back to the task at hand. "Why don't you print out a copy, Jen?"

I could feel my heart pumping with excitement as I printed out the recipe for our Gooey Good Caramel Apples. I really believed people would buy them. Lots of them.

Maybe there was a chance I wouldn't be wearing pajamas to school, after all.

"Those will be easy to make," Felicia said.

"Okay, that's one snack," Marc said.

"Two, if you count the s'mores," Josh pointed out. I laughed. That was Josh, always precise with the numbers.

"We need more!" Carolyn exclaimed.

"And the sweeter the better," Marilyn added.

"How about cotton candy?" Rachel suggested. "It's pure sugar. Nothing's sweeter than that."

Caramel Apples

INGREDIENTS:

6 small apples, 1 14-oz package of caramels, ½ cup chopped peanuts, 6 Popsicle sticks

DIRECTIONS:

1. Line a cookie sheet with waxed paper. Empty the nuts onto the paper in six equal piles. Leave at least six inches between each pile of nuts.
2. Wash and dry the apples. Twist off the stems and push a Popsicle stick halfway into each apple in the spot where the stem used to be.
3. Ask an adult to help you melt the caramels in a saucepan over low heat.
4. Dip apples in the melted caramel. Use a knife to cover the whole apple in caramel.
5. Place each apple, stick side up, onto a heap of nuts and roll over to cover.
6. Refrigerate the apples until the caramel is firm. This usually takes about half an hour.

Josh shook his head. "I think you need a special machine to make cotton candy. And the school would never give us the money to rent one."

"Then how about popcorn?" Liza suggested. "We could buy the packaged kind."

"Better yet, how about popcorn *balls*?" I asked, as I opened an online recipe called Perfect Popcorn Balls.

"You mean those sticky, sweet, gooey things that always get stuck between your teeth?" Chloe asked, making a face.

"Yeah," I answered, sounding less confident. Maybe they weren't such a good idea. If Chloe didn't . . .

Just then, a broad smile broke out across Chloe's face. "Perfect! I like popcorn balls a lot!" she exclaimed. Then, looking at my surprised expression, she added, "Gotcha!"

I stuck my tongue out at her, but I had to laugh. "Yeah, you did," I admitted.

"I *love* popcorn balls," Marilyn said.

"That goes double for me," Carolyn added.

"*Everything* goes double for you guys," Marc teased the twins.

"Okay, popcorn balls it is," I said, clicking the printer icon.

"This all sounds delicious," Sam said, scanning the recipe as it came out of the printer. "And we're going to have such fun cooking them together. We can work at my

Perfect Popcorn Balls

INGREDIENTS:

1 regular-size package of microwave popcorn, ½ cup dark corn syrup, ½ cup sugar, ½ teaspoon salt, a few tablespoons butter

DIRECTIONS:

1. Place the package of popcorn in your microwave. Follow the popping directions on the package to set the timer on your microwave.
2. While the corn is popping, mix together corn syrup, sugar, and salt.
3. Place the popped popcorn in a large kettle.
4. With the help of an adult, pour the corn syrup, salt, and sugar mixture into the popcorn. Continue stirring and tossing the popcorn constantly over medium heat for 3 to 5 minutes, or until the sugar is dissolved and the popcorn is evenly coated with the mixture.
5. Remove the kettle from heat. Allow the popcorn mixture to cool slightly before handling it.
6. Spread butter over clean hands, and gently form the popcorn into balls.

Makes about a dozen popcorn balls.

house if you like. My mum's a great cook and I know she'd help us."

"Sounds good to me," Chloe said. "But we've got to get moving on this. The carnival is a week from Sunday."

"I don't have any after-school activities," Sam told her. "So I can cook any day. But the rest of you are so busy. Let's try to find a day when we can all get together, and I'll call my mum and let her know."

I was seriously impressed as I watched Sam and my friends compare calendars to find a free afternoon to make our carnival treats. Sam had only been hanging out with my friends and me for less than one day, but already she had managed to become one of us. Not a leader. Or a trendsetter. Just one of the crowd. And from the smile on her face, I could tell that was what she'd been hoping for all along.

Chapter NINE

"LOOK WHAT JOSH WON FOR ME!" Felicia exclaimed excitedly, running over to our booth with a small, green teddy bear in her arms. "He guessed exactly how many jelly beans were in the jar! It was unbelievable, Jenny. He did all of these calculations based on the size of the jar and the average size of a jelly bean, and then added them up in his head."

"And look what Felicia won for me," Josh added, coming up behind her. He was carrying a huge black-and-white stuffed panda. The plush toy was so massive I could barely see his eyes peering out from behind it. "You should have seen her. She was amazing. She knocked down the milk bottle pyramid on the first try at the baseball toss."

I grinned. Josh and Felicia were so perfect for each other. And, like everyone else at the school carnival, they were having a great time. The carnival was mobbed with people. We were going to raise a lot of money for the kids who were affected by the earthquake. It's really impressive what middle school kids can do in three weeks when they put their minds to it.

I had spent the whole morning at The Sports Café, so I hadn't gotten a chance to play any games yet. I hadn't gotten to see how long the lines were over at the Pops' makeover photo booth, either. I was almost afraid to ask if they were making a lot of money. But I just had to know. "So, um, did you guys happen to pass by Addie's booth?" I asked finally.

Felicia and Josh looked at each other and didn't say anything for a moment. Finally, Felicia admitted, "It's pretty crowded over there, Jen."

Josh glanced at the long line of people waiting to shoot hoops and buy a snack at our booth. "But I don't think it's as mobbed as our booth is," he said. "For starters, we have both boys and girls here. And then, if you figure the average person takes up a cubic area of . . ."

"Never mind," I interrupted him. "There's no point figuring out all that now. We won't know who really won the bet until we count the money at the end of the day."

"Exactly," Felicia said. "And people sure are buying a lot of food. I saw a lot of folks walking around with popcorn balls and caramel apples."

"Not to mention chocolate-and-marshmallow-covered faces and fingers," Josh added. "Our s'mores have created a lot of sticky messes out there!"

"Good!" I exclaimed. "That's what I want to hear."

Just then, Marc came running over to us, his camera in hand. "Did you guys see who just bought a bunch of popcorn balls and caramel apples?" he asked, as he continued to film the people in line for his documentary.

I followed his camera angle, and caught a glimpse

of Dana, Maya, and Claire all paying for snacks at The Sports Café!

"Oooh, Addie's not going to like that," Felicia predicted.

Boy, was she right! A moment later, the great Addie Wilson herself came storming over to our booth. "What are you doing?" she demanded angrily of her friends.

"We were hungry," Maya explained.

"Couldn't you have found somewhere else to get food?" Addie asked.

Claire shook her head. "They have the only snack booth at the whole carnival." She took a bite of her caramel apple. "This is really delish. You want a bite, Ad?"

Addie looked like she was about to explode. "No, I do *not* want a bite!" she shouted. Then, after realizing that people were watching (and filming!) her, she quieted down. "Do you guys want to win the bet or not?" she asked Dana, Maya, and Claire.

Dana shrugged and pulled a piece of sticky popcorn from her popcorn ball. "It's your bet, Addie, not ours. I don't know why you made it anyway."

Wow. I couldn't believe Dana had just said that. Here my friends were all volunteering to wear pajamas to school with me if I lost the bet, and Dana – Addie's *supposedly* new best friend – was completely abandoning her.

Sam had been right. The Pops sure were a two-faced group. Which was probably why they stuck together – who else would want friends like that?

"Hi, Addie!" I heard Sam's voice pop up over the noise

of the crowd. "So glad you stopped by. Do you want to buy a s'more? They're really scrumptious."

"Oooh, I didn't know you had s'mores," Dana said. "How much . . ." She stopped as Addie elbowed her in the side. "Ouch. What was that for?" she asked her.

"No, we don't want any more food," Addie insisted, turning away from Sam and starting back to her booth. "Come on, you guys," she said to Dana, Maya, and Claire. "We need help back at our booth. We're much busier than they are here."

I knew she had added that last part for my benefit, and I worked really hard not to look like I was worried – even though I was.

As the Pops walked away, Dana said really loudly, "Chocolate makes you break out, anyway. No one should eat s'mores unless they want a face full of pimples."

"Yeah, you should come over to our booth and have your picture taken – before you break out," Claire added.

I frowned. Great. Now I was afraid everyone would stop buying the s'mores. And up until now they had been our bestsellers.

But they didn't stop buying them. No one left our booth to go over to the Pops' photo booth. No one listened to Dana and Claire at all. Obviously, people liked chocolate more than they liked the Pops. It was like chocolate was the Pops' kryptonite.

Which was not to say that the Pops' booth was empty.

Not by a long shot. As I walked past it on my break from The Sports Café, I could see a long line of people waiting to be made over by the trendsetters of Joyce Kilmer Middle School.

No doubt about it. This bet was going to be close. So who was going to be wearing her pajamas to school tomorrow? We wouldn't know until the last dime was counted. Suddenly I felt kind of sick to my stomach. And I knew it wasn't because I'd had too many popcorn balls!

Everyone in C wing stopped what they were doing and stared. They pointed. A few people gasped. But mostly they just stared.

"Pajamas? To school?" someone exclaimed with surprise.

"Is that allowed?" another person asked.

Chloe came up beside me and wrapped her arm over my shoulder. "Bet you're glad that's not you," she whispered in my ear.

"You have no idea," I agreed. There was no way anyone could imagine how excited I had been late Sunday afternoon when all the money had finally been counted and I'd learned our booth had earned seventy-three dollars more than the Pops' booth had. We'd won the bet by a lot more than I'd ever dreamed!

But that feeling was nothing compared to the relief I was experiencing now while I watched as Addie – and not me – walked down the hall in her pajamas.

"I'm really glad you won the bet, Jenny," Chloe told me.

I shook my head. "*We* won the bet," I corrected her. "There's no way I could have done it alone."

"That's true," Chloe agreed. "It took Liza's artwork, Felicia's sports expertise, the twins' cooking talents, Josh's budgeting, Sam's love of American food, and my brilliant organizational skills to pull it off."

"Hey, don't I get any credit?" I asked her.

Chloe laughed. "Your bet spurred us on to do great things," she joked.

"Oh that's just brill!" Sam exclaimed as she walked up beside Chloe and me. "There goes Addie in her pajama top and trousers."

"Thanks to your sweet tooth, it's not me," I told her. "It was your idea to add a café to our basketball booth, remember? That was sheer brilliance. Thank you."

"Oh, cheers, mate," Sam said with a grin. "I mean, you're welcome, friend," she corrected herself in her best imitation of an American accent – which wasn't very good. "It was fun, wasn't it? And seeing Addie strutting around in her pajamas is absolutely the icing on the cake."

We all looked over toward Addie. She was heading to English class. Her head was held high, and she'd fastened a smile onto her lips, but I could tell she was uncomfortable. Of course, having Marc follow her down the hall with his video camera wasn't making it any easier for her.

"He's definitely getting his comic relief for the documentary," Chloe said as she observed the whole scene.

But Chloe was wrong. People didn't seem to find Addie padding down the hall in blue-and-white-flannel bunny pajamas particularly funny. Not one person was laughing at her. In fact, people seemed sort of impressed.

"She's totally got guts," I heard one girl say. "I heard about the bet, but I didn't think either one of them would ever go through with it."

"I have to ask her where she got those pajamas," another girl noted. "They'd be perfect for the sleepover party I'm going to."

"Wearing pajamas isn't a bad idea," a third girl suggested. "It sure would help me get to school on time if I didn't have to get dressed in the morning."

Wow. It didn't seem to matter what Addie wore or did. In the end, she wound up setting the trends. I had a feeling that within a week everyone would be wearing pajamas to school. Okay, so that was an exaggeration, but you know what I mean.

"Well, we'd better get going," Sam said. "Ms. Jaffe gets so angry when we're late."

"Seriously," Chloe said. "I don't need another late on my report card. My mother will have a fit."

And with that, everything went back to normal. My friends and I rushed off to class, pretty much unnoticed by everyone else in the hallway. And Addie walked through the halls being noticed and admired by everyone.

Still, looking over at Chloe and Sam, I was reminded of how supportive all of my friends had been through this whole thing. And that made me realize something very important.

I wouldn't have it any other way.

Cheerio Isn't Always a Cereal

English is English, right? Well, not exactly. The truth is, Americans and Britons don't always speak the same language. How well could you communicate with a kid from across the pond? Take this English-English quiz and find out.

(Relax – this quiz won't count toward your English grade on your next report card. It's just for fun!)

1. If your British pal is just "mucking around," what's she doing?

A. Goofing off
B. Taking a hike in the mud
C. Doing homework

2. If you're in England and you see a black-and-white sign, what should you do?

A. Keep an eye out for zebras. After all, you are at the zoo.
B. Look both ways — you're at a crosswalk.
C. Open up your wallet — you're at the cool new shop in the mall that only sells things in black and white.

3. **What is a lollipop man?**

A. The candy vendor at the mall

B. A pocketbook

C. A crossing guard

4. **True or False: Lorry is a British nickname for a boy named Laurence.**

5. **You're on the lookout for a new jumper. What are you searching for?**

A. A jump rope

B. A trampoline

C. A sweater

6. **Time for a fresh nappy! Can you guess what that is?**

A. A short mid-afternoon sleep

B. A clean baby diaper

C. A sugar cookie

7. Uh-oh! You just found out you have a math test in a fortnight. How long do you have to study?

A. Two weeks
B. One week
C. Twenty-four hours

8. True or false: A dressing gown is the perfect outfit for a formal royal ball.

9. Where should you carry a torch?

A. At the Statue of Liberty
B. In the woods at night
C. At a firehouse

10. What's a fairy cake?

A. A cake you leave for the tooth fairy
B. Angel food cake
C. A cupcake

Now Check Your Answers:

1. A
2. B
3. C: British crossing guards are called "lollipop men" because the stop signs they carry look like giant lollipops.
4. False: Lorry is the British word for truck.
5. C
6. B
7. A
8. False: Dressing gown is the British term for bathrobe. (You might be able to wear one to a fancy royal sleepover, though. ☺)
9. B: A torch is an English-English word for flashlight.
10. C

So how English is your English?

8–10 correct: Cheers! This high score is really brill! (That's how the British say amazing!)

4–7 correct: This score really rates, mate. You're getting the hang of it.

0–3 correct: Ouch. You're going to need some more education before you can speak English the way the English do. You can study while you snack on fish and chips.